D0714245

Playing Against the Odds

by

Bernard Ashley

Illustrated by Derek Brazell

First published in Great Britain by Barrington Stoke Ltd
10 Belford Terrace, Edinburgh EH4 3DQ
Copyright © 2000 Bernard Ashley
Illustrations © Derek Brazell
The moral right of the author has been asserted in
accordance with the Copyright, Designs and
Patents Act 1988
ISBN 1-902260-69-4
Printed by Polestar AUP Aberdeen Ltd

The publisher gratefully acknowledges general subsidy
from the Scottish Arts Council towards the Barrington Stoke
teenage fiction series

THE SCOTTISH ARTS COUNCIL

A Note from the Author

I moved from London to Kent, from town to country when I was 13. I had to change schools and I felt awful about it. I had to leave all my old friends behind. It is hard to stand in front of a strange class, feeling different and to know that everyone is staring at you. That year was not a good time for me.

The feelings I had then inspired this story - but I've made some changes. The new girl in the form is really me but instead of moving from London to Kent, the girl in the story moves from north to south. However, there's still the same sense of being an outsider.

This book is for insiders and outsiders everywhere.

Contents

Chris

Fiona

The
Form Room

Chapter 1
Christopher Sinclair Foreman

Christopher Sinclair Foreman.
Christopher S. Foreman. Chris Foreman.
C. S. Foreman. Sinclair Foreman.
C. Sinclair Foreman. CSF. The names,
they're all OK, I reckon.

I suppose it's a sort of gift, to like the
sound of your own name. Which is not the

way I'd feel if I was Roland Butter or
C. Shaw. Not the way at all.

Although when you know them, people
become people and their names just fit
them.

Chrissy Foreman. That's the only name
I wouldn't take. The urge to say Cissy
Chrissy is the big danger there – unless
you're the best fighter in the form. Which
I'm not.

See, I mustn't damage my hands,
fighting. I'm doing my Grade Seven piano
exam at Easter.

They're all talking at home as if I've got
it already. Head down and practise,

practise, practise. Which I don't mind so long as I don't have to miss football for it.

****

Getting my head down is just what it is, because I have got a fight on my hands against my own stupid body. It's playing me up so badly. It's doing these things I don't want just because a new girl's come into the form and she's been put next to me.

This Fiona Radcliffe comes in on Monday talking all northern. She stands up at the front while Mr Henshaw makes a fish supper out of what she's saying. He pretends he can't understand a word. And she gets me going, feeling sorry for her and something more besides. You know — when you get that tingle on your skin and you start breathing like you're out of breath.

The stupid thing is, it's only because she's new. She's not someone I've known since I was three like the rest of the girls. So she's not someone I don't notice any more.

Fiona Radcliffe. A living, breathing female with a face and hair and skin. Quite a lot of skin showing, to be fair.

And Henshaw's put her to sit next to me for registration. As he's the Music teacher he chooses where we sit like he's setting out an orchestra.

I'm a first violin. A red-faced one. In fact with this new female so close I've started going red all over the place. Well, not all over the place, I don't think. I haven't checked. There's no way you can in public. But definitely on my face, the part of me everyone can see.

I get so dry in the mouth that I could do with a bottle of water to sip all the time. Perhaps it's my body trying to sort out the going red.

The other trouble is, she's only been here a day and suddenly there's a nuclear explosion.

After dinner Andy, the new assistant caretaker, is being shown round the Music

Room (which is also our form room) and told the rules about the instruments.

All at once Lucy Brewer gets out of her pram! She's lost her christening ring. She has to take it off for PE and she's been putting it in her locker all the year. At the end of the morning it was in her locker. This afternoon it's not. Who's the ratbag thief, she wants to know.

Weird or what? This new girl walks in and a thief walks in with her?

And just my luck, I'm sitting next to her. Right next, like she's my partner and so close I can smell her skin. Peaches, I think. Or is it pears? And thinking about it, I suddenly start going red again.

So keep your head down and concentrate on your Grade Seven, C. Sinclair Foreman!

Chapter 2
New Girl, Stolen Ring

But now I'm sitting at the piano in our front room and I'm definitely not giving my fingering much thought.

I'm thinking about Fiona. About registration. She looked really proud standing there while Henshaw put her onto the register. Most people mumble and crawl with Henshaw because he's so strict. But she stood and faced him out. When he pretended he couldn't understand her, she spelt the words out in a clear, loud voice. And that's got me too, the way she talks.

A lot of people in our form talk with different accents. They're mostly Asian cockney or docklands Afro-Caribbean. But this girl from the north talks with different vowels. She says 'coom' instead of 'come' and 'tek' instead of 'take'. She uses different words, too. We say 'coach' and she says 'boos'. The way it comes out of her mouth it sort of sings. I like the sound and I like her mouth too.

So I'm playing the piano. Left hand, get it right! I'm thinking of Fiona's mouth and of kissing it. Which I mustn't or Mum and

Dad'll hear me going red. So many wrong notes.

But I can't get her out of my head. I think about that first day. The rest of the girls looked at her as if she'd been raked up off the muck heap. You can see them nudging and twisting and muttering. That hair! That short skirt! Those bare legs!

They stare ice at her while I go hot in the face. And the blokes are so basic. They eye her up and down as if she's something on the front of the *Daily Sport*. When she's told to sit next to me and I shift up to let her in, they all start making these faces like monkeys pouting for bananas.

That was her first morning. Then after the dinner break Lucy Brewer screams like there's a mouse in her locker. She starts shouting in this high wail and going on about this christening ring she's lost.

"That's two octaves too high," says Henshaw, all sarky. "Come down to middle C, girl and I'll listen to you."

Lucy Brewer looks like she's going to hit him. She has hit a teacher once before. When she got into trouble for it, her Dad came up and hit the teacher, too.

So Henshaw soon starts taking some notes. Lucy's gold ring has gone in spite of the *No Jewellery* rule. She claims she has the right to wear it. After all, the Sikh boys can wear their kara bangles. She takes it off every PE and Games lesson and puts it in her locker, the way the rest of us take off our watches and park our mobiles.

And the ring's gone. Definitely gone.
"Has anyone seen it?" asks Henshaw.

"Only when she was wearing it," some
idiot says.

Then Henshaw suddenly turns on Fiona.
"What about you?" he asks, heavy as the law
stopping a crook with a bag marked 'swag'.
What Henshaw doesn't say is what
everyone is thinking. New girl. Stolen ring.
Nothing gone missing before. Got to be her.

Fiona suddenly stands up next to me
and I get a whiff of her perfume. She stares
across at Lucy Brewer, then at Henshaw.
"Y'want to search me?" she asks and all the
lads groan.

Chapter 3
Ten to One, Guilty

There are others who could have stolen the ring. Nicky Drew's Dad's doing time for theft. Nicky's scared of him. But I reckon Nicky's a victim not a thief.

Sally Booth used to be a little magpie at primary school. She could have stolen it.

No one who knows Lucy Brewer is likely to want to upset her ...

So the fingers do point at someone new. And that's Fiona Radcliffe.

I agree. When I see her again the next day I go short of breath and my mouth's dry. But I still take a quick look at her fingers to see if she's wearing a ring. As if she'd be so stupid!

She has her hands laid on the desk top like an advert for skin cream and her fingers are bare. White. Long fingers. Nails slightly sparkly but clear. She has a pianist's fingers and do I fancy playing a duet! Sensitive, nimble fingers that could be into a locker and out in no time.

Then it happens again! Another theft. This time it's something of Drew Sutton's – he's football captain and the middle of our back four. Again, no one robs Drew Sutton unless they're wanting hospital.

He's gone straight to his locker to get the organiser he left there last night and comes away shouting, "Prat!"

"Who are you calling a prat, Sutton, me or one of your classmates?" Henshaw can be a real pain.

"Someone's nicked my organiser!" yells Drew.

"Then you should organise your organiser better. Did you leave it in your locker?" asks Henshaw.

"Yeah," answered Drew.

"*Yeah,* what?"

"Yeah, I left it in my locker. An' now it's flaming gone!"

Henshaw shakes his head, like he's never understood the stupidity of idiots who leave things in their own personal locked lockers. What the hell are lockers for?

And Lucy Brewer's brought a note from her father to say that the school has got to pay for her ring. It's worth £500.

Even that wouldn't ruffle up Henshaw to do more than report the thefts to the Head of Year. Then all that changes suddenly when one of his precious instruments goes missing too.

Rachel Searle plays flute in the school orchestra. Flutes are expensive, so she has a school one on long-term loan. And when she comes in she tells him it went missing last night from the cloakroom. While she went for a pee after the rehearsal.

"Yesterday! Overnight! Why have things suddenly taken such a turn for the worse?" Henshaw looks across at Fiona Radcliffe sitting next to me. "A term and a half with no trouble, then, *Surprise Symphony*, we have a thief in our midst!"

I can hear Fiona breathe in hard. I can sense her next to me, as if she's giving out a vibration.

I look down, away from everyone's eyes. I see her knees parting and closing, parting and closing like she's all tensed up. Private movements, just for her but shared with me.

It makes me feel special. And I remember what I don't want to. I remember what she said yesterday about being searched. And with everyone's eyes staring our way, things start happening down below the desk that should never happen in a form room.

No!

I sweat. I pray that Fiona won't look down. I wish that demon dead. I start going over the left hand of *Piano Intermezzo* in my head, setting it to the words of the seventeen times table.

If Henshaw makes me stand up, I'm going to get a round of applause. But while I sweat he says, "I shall arrange for this room to be locked at all times when it's empty. You will line up outside. You cannot be trusted. Anyone allowed in here for practice or study will have to be with a responsible partner. That's called prevention. Meanwhile we'll investigate high and low. That flute is worth £200."

"My ring's worth £500!" yells Lucy.

"My organiser's top of the range …" Drew reminds everyone.

Henshaw ignores all this. He's in real Sherlock Holmes form now. "But first a search …" He orders everyone to open their lockers which are across the back of the room. Then everyone has to stand at their desks with the contents of their bags set out before them.

By then, thank goodness, my personal problem has gone down.

The interest is enormous as Henshaw goes round. It's a real eye-opener, what's in people's lockers and bags. A couple of lads try to hide biological magazines that don't quite cover the syllabus. One of the girls finds a doughnut from the last millennium. And Drew Sutton – of all people – has got a teddy bear that he swears is an exam mascot.

But there's no ring, no organiser and no flute. Somehow, I knew there wouldn't be. If Fiona Radcliffe is a thief, she strikes me as the clever sort.

We go off to our lessons with everyone talking about nicking. Everyone looks at Fiona Radcliffe like an Old Bailey jury. As we cram out through the classroom door, Lucy Brewer goes right up to her and says, "Why don't you come clean, you northern cow!"

Fiona gets pushed about a lot. Henshaw isn't too quick to stop it as he comes back with the assistant caretaker to lock the door.

Is she guilty or not? I don't know, but I've got my suspicions.

One thing's clear though, my body's telling me that I am. Guilty. That agony under the desk has given me that message. Nothing like this was going on before she came.

She may be a thief but if she is, I'm guilty of falling for one.

Whichever lesson or room we're in and wherever we're sitting, I know where Fiona is and what she's doing, every minute. I keep taking quick looks at her all the time, check, check, check, check, check.

I know her face so well. Her high forehead, her brushed back hair and her pony tail, her little nose, her smooth throat, her slender neck, her greeny blue eyes and her serious mouth.

Serious! I'll say serious. See what I mean? I lie in bed and I have to say I have fantasies about kissing that mouth. But that's all, honestly. I don't know why the thing happened under the desk because that's not the sort of way I think about Fiona. Not the crude way the lads go on. It's something sweeter.

But it's just such a rotten shame that ten-to-one she's a thief.

Chapter 4
Lock the Form Room Door

I have regular piano practice at school. My piano teacher works at the school so I'm allowed to use a school piano. I practise every Monday, Wednesday and Thursday, from 12:30 to one o'clock, on the upright piano in the Music Room.

Never on the Steinway grand. That's got a cover over it like a horse in winter, unless Henshaw's at it himself. But the upright's kept in tune and the keys are regularly wiped down.

And there I sit, three lunchtimes a week, on my own, unless someone's sitting at one of the desks finishing off work. Not that there is often anyone there. Who wants to finish work with me doing scales, when they can be in the library with the computers and having a laugh?

That Wednesday morning I clear it with Henshaw that I can still get into the Music Room to practise. Nothing's gone missing overnight. It looks as if locking the form room door is working. But I do need to be let in. I want to get that Grade Seven.

"All arranged!" Henshaw sings, as smug as ever. "The caretaker chappie will lock up after you at one o'clock."

All I have to do is stay on in there when the last lesson finishes at 12:30. I turn away.

"And you've got a responsible partner," he goes on.

I hadn't forgotten.

"The new girl's writing up lesson notes from last half term. They're years behind, up north," he continued.

Talk about prejudice.

But now I'm all in a state of bubbles-in-the-blood about the lunch hour. How can I practise with Fiona Radcliffe sitting there! I'd gone to sleep thinking about her and woken up after a dream about her which I won't go into. And today I'm going to be in the form room on my own with her. Trying to practise for Grade Seven?

Oh, lock the form room door!

****

As the rest go out at the end of the morning I get the expected remarks. So-called funny.

"Nail your music down, Foreman."

"Keep both hands on the piano, son!"

"We can hear you outside!"

Fiona takes no notice of them. She's over at her desk sorting out her ballpoint and her books. I don't look at her but I know what she's doing. I know every move she makes.

I go to the piano and raise the lid. I put my music on the stand. I lay my fingers gently on the keys – and totally ignore the music sheet.

I play the *Thief of Love* theme which I know by heart. My Dad isn't into music but he sits and listens to that piece when I play it and always claps at the end. Even if I play it three times running, he claps each time. My Grade Seven's for him, partly.

But playing it today is a signal being sent out. This is something I hadn't planned. And, signal received, Fiona comes across the room to the piano.

"Is tha' what you're training up?"

"What?" I carry on playing while I reply, looking round at her like some idiot in a film. I don't go wrong, either, not on the notes. But my 'touch' is all over the place, loud where it should be soft, soft where it should be loud. Trembly where it should be firm.

"It's great!"

"It's gross," I tell her.

"Shall I turn your music?" Now she's got a hand on the book. "But I can't read it. Ye'll have to nod at me."

She hasn't noticed I've not been using the music. I smile and turn to say I don't need it. And where her hand is stretched out at the music I see into her short sleeve. And there's the edge of a bra.

I go so hot I could heat the school. I go so dry it's like a mouthful of moths. I go so weak I couldn't lift a lettuce. And my stomach is a cage of fluttering wings.

Stupid! I've seen bras before. I've seen bare boobs before on holiday. After the first day you don't take any notice. But this is different. This is like seeing the private Fiona. And I have the privilege of being the only one.

She's moved closer now to turn the sheet and I realise she's leaning against me. I should work the loud pedal but I don't want to move my leg.

"I'm not reading the music," I get out somehow.

"No?"

But she doesn't move – not her hand, not her arm, not her leg. I play on, the cronkiest playing of the *Thief of Love* anyone's likely to hear. When I get to the end, I start straight away again from the beginning. I don't want this moment to go away.

And it doesn't. Great kid, she stays just like that while I play it through again.

When I've finished this time, Fiona asks, "Do you know this?" She sits on the stool, shares it. "Shove up." And she plays *Chopsticks*.

I play it, too, up at my end.

"That's all I can do," she says.

"It's good," I tell her.

"It's crap!" Fiona turns and looks at me. Her face has never been this close to mine. "Like this crap school!"

"Why d'you come here?" I ask, our hands are still resting on the keyboard, with a touch of little fingers that neither of us move. And I look down to see what note we're touching on. Because my first piano concerto is going to be written round that note.

"We came down 'cos of him! Our Dad. Went off wi' his office cleaner. Me an' me mam's come down to live wi' an auntie while we get put on the 'ousing list ..."

"Ah."

And suddenly she stands up. "Ye'd better get on. Me bum's goin' numb. But you're ace at piano, Chrissy, I tell ya."

Chrissy! She called me 'Chrissy' which I never ever thought could sound OK. But, God, does it! I can't wait to get home to go over all this in my head. I've never been this close to a girl except in a play fight. I've never had someone talk to me like this, as if they really give a damn about me.

Fiona goes and gets on with her work and I get on with my piano practice. I do have to do some scales. I'm not what you'd call fluent. Every time I make a mistake she calls out, "Hey!" So she's still noticing me then.

At one o'clock Andy, the new caretaker, is at the door, all rattling keys. We pack up and go our separate ways.

But before we do, Fiona asks, "When's your next practice, Chrissy?"

"Tomorrow."

"Poor old you!" she says. "Me wi' all this catchin' up to do. Ye're goin' to get pestered wi' me again ..."

"Never mind," I say. "I'll survive."

Which I might, just.

Chapter 5
Grass!

I'm riding my bike round the park but I don't know where I'm going. I just don't want to be in the house where ordinary life is going on. I want to be on my own for a think.

Because that afternoon after the piano practice, Linda Forth finds she's lost her pen. It's a good one, a Parker. She's been stupid and left it on her desk at 12:30. After lunch it's gone and who'd been in the form room meanwhile? Me and Fiona Radcliffe.

I know I didn't take it. The others start pointing fingers at me, but I turn all my stuff out. I offer to go to the bogs with Drew Sutton to let him look where no man dares.

But it's soon clear the spotlight's not on me. It's Fiona Radcliffe they suspect. She'd been in at lunchtime, too and she'd had half an hour afterwards to hide the pen. And I've got to say, she was working near Linda Forth's desk. Once I was doing scales my eyes were not quite so fixed on all her movements.

I've got to think about this. Because I do like Fiona. I do get a tingle on my skin when I suddenly see her. I do go upside down inside when someone says her name. If my Mum said 'Fiona Radcliffe' indoors I'd have to dive under the table and die.

But she's probably a common thief.

In the end I just get off my bike and sit in the park, on the grass.

Of course, Fiona and her Mum are up against it. Leaving Bolton, living with an auntie, they must be short of dosh. If Fiona can sell the things she's stolen, she can help out with the housekeeping, can't she?

I sit and I think. My backside goes numb and I think of what Fiona said, when we

41

were sitting on the piano stool. About her numb bum. I think of her touch and her face up close to mine.

In my head I kiss her and I stroke her bare arm. And she starts to cry and she tells me all about the stealing. She says she's only been trying to help her Mum but now she wants to put things right. Meeting a straight guy like Chrissy Foreman has shown her how stupid she'd be to spoil everything – getting excluded and having to go to another school ...

And I hug her and tell her I'll help. If she gives all the stolen stuff to me, I'll get it back to where it belongs and we can start again.

And she thanks me and kisses me deeper.

And now I know what a romantic daydream is.

I'm going to face her with this tomorrow. It's got to get sorted.

I always know where she is. Fiona stands out for me in the yard next morning like an 'ever-glo' statue. I'm over by the gate and she's over by the entrance to the school, well before it's time to go in.

As I'm watching her, she looks round the yard and sort of slips in through the door like a ... like a burglar. Then a few minutes later she comes running out and goes to stand over by the fence. It's as if she's been standing there all the time.

Why did she go in? To go to the loo? Those doors are all unlocked. The cleaners and the teachers are all around before school starts so the form room doors are unlocked, too. And Henshaw goes in to polish his piano keys.

So why should I be surprised when we're all sitting there for registration and Henshaw suddenly flips his lid? Literally. The lid of his piano. The Steinway. The cover's off, the lid's up and he's rooting about inside.

"It's not here! It's not here!" he yells, like the chorus of one of his school musicals.

It's where he keeps his Filofax during the day. I didn't know that. It's got his credit cards and concert tickets in it. Each morning he gets in early and puts his valuables in a safe place.

Has Fiona Radcliffe sussed that too? Was that why she slipped in early?

Anyway, registration is like the crash, bang of the *1812 Overture* – cannons booming, brass blaring, the organ with all its stops out. Someone's got in before school and been under his piano lid!

Fiona looks at me and she's as red as I usually am. She's lost her cool now, all right. She looks as guilty as hell. I could have sorted the other stuff for her, but I can't get the Filofax back to Henshaw.

"Right!" he screams, all soprano. "I want lockers left open. Put your bags on your

desks again, then everyone to the Library.
This is a police matter. Fingerprints,
everything."

"DNA testing, sir?" asks Bernie Mulligan.
"We got to give body fluids?"

"Anything to catch and convict the
thief!" says Henshaw. He's looking laser
sharp at Fiona Radcliffe. And you could see
he'd bring back the death penalty or
transportation to Australia for nicking his
tickets to the Proms.

You can hear the mutter, mutter,
mutter, mutter as everyone trails to the
Library. Fiona Radcliffe is definitely ten
degrees less cool than before. But as we're
walking along the corridor, she gets herself
tucked in next to me.

"Did ye get it?" she says, low and very serious.

"No!" I say. "Get what?"

"It's in your cubby. I put it there a'fore school. Ye did get it out?"

"No, I didn't!" I tell her.

"Oh, 'ell!" she says.

I pull myself away from Fiona like a magnet turned the wrong way round. I've got to get as far away from her as possible!

We all stand around in the Library, waiting for instructions. Then the Deputy Head comes in to tell us to go to our Maths

47

sets. It's clear that no one's got Henshaw's Filofax on them. We can carry on for now.

And all through maths I'm weak inside, with fear. They're going to find Henshaw's Filofax with my stuff. Fiona Radcliffe's nicked it and put it in my locker! And wasn't I alone with her yesterday when the pen went missing? We could have hatched this plot then. Which isn't true but who's to know that?

She misread the message when I played the *Thief of Love* music. I said *Love*, but she heard *Thief.* She thought I wanted in on the stealing.

And still she looks really beautiful across the room. I'm in the sort of twist you wouldn't wish on a tornado.

But I'm me and I'm innocent. Stop practising piano at school? The Grade Seven exam off, blown out of the window? No way!

And I think of my Dad getting that news. I think of the look on his face.

So at the bell for break I do what I have to do. I lose myself from the form and get back to the Music room and Henshaw.

He's waiting for the police. "Yes?" he asks. He looks dead white and I wonder what else he had in his Filofax. Lady harpists' addresses?

I mumble and mutter. But at last I get it out. "I saw Fiona Radcliffe coming into school early," I tell him. He just stares at me. "And I think she might have put something in my locker."

Still Henshaw stares. Then he says. "Thank you."

And I have to go. I trip on my laces and fumble at the door handle.

And I feel like the biggest heel in the world. How dare I have daydreams about Fiona Radcliffe? I'm a traitor! I've never felt about anyone the way I feel about her.

She gives me the biggest buzz. I've had the best thoughts anyone could have about her. And I've grassed her up.

But who said life had to be simple? I had to do what I had to do. I had to be fair to myself. I wouldn't have ratted on her to help anyone else.

All the same, I've dropped her right in it – the girl I reckon I love ...

Chapter 6
Love Letter

There's no piano practice after the lunch hour, because the CID's in there.

The place looks like there's been a drugs bust. There's stuff everywhere, heaped up on our desks. All the lockers are empty, their doors swung open like the first day of term.

No one touches anything. After the
search the day before there's nothing
shaming to cover up. Drew's teddy must be
safe at home on his pillow.

I sit next to Fiona as if the icy Moscow
river runs between us. I'm giving her my
back. I don't want to see any part of her. I
don't want anything to turn my stomach
over with love.

I tell myself her face is pretty ugly,
when you think about it. Well, not ugly, but
very ordinary. And everyone's got legs,
arms and skin. Half the people in school
wear bras. And isn't there a sort of whine
in her voice all the time?

So why did I ever think Fiona was
anyone special? What a fool I've been! Look

at all the trouble she's caused.

Then she leans over and whispers in my ear. A warm, soft whisper and I groan inside. I've just been kidding myself.

"It's all all right, then, Chrissy, loov."

She pats a pink envelope on the top of my pile of personal belongings. I haven't noticed it up till then.

But before I have to reply to her, or get to look at it, Henshaw stands up to get our attention. He waves both arms to draw us in. He looks as if he's about to conduct us in the Hallelujah Chorus.

"I'm relieved to tell you all, the case is closed. I won't go into it – I can't – but the thief in the school has been laid bare."

"Strip-searched, sir?" asks Bernie Mulligan.

Guff, guff, guff. And everyone looks at Fiona Radcliffe. Everyone except me. Because my neck is so stiff and brittle my head would fall off if I turned it round.

Henshaw shakes his head. "No, Mulligan, that wasn't necessary. But it did get to fingerprints ..."

Henshaw looks round the room. It's like he knows he can't say anything, but he's telling us some other way. He nods his head at various places where there's white fingerprint powder dusted about. The

locker doors, the piano lid on the grand.
And the window pole.

I take a quick look down at Fiona's
hands. You don't get that black police ink
off your fingers in a hurry, I bet. And
they're still long, slender and clean.

But Henshaw's look is fixed on the
window pole. *Window pole* he's saying with
his eyes. Window pole! What's special about
the window pole?

And we twig it.

Who's allowed to use the window pole?
For Health and Safety, who's the only
person allowed to open and shut the top
windows? Not even the staff. It has to be

the caretaking people. They have to send for Mr Brown or his new assistant, Andy.

Andy! Who came new to the school the same day as Fiona did! Andy!

Everyone starts asking Henshaw if it's Andy, but he can't say. He's got *no comment* written all over his face. His lips are firmly sealed with that little smirk that says he knows a semi quaver from a demi-semi quaver!

It was the new assistant caretaker! It wasn't Fiona at all. Fiona Radcliffe is as innocent as the day that she was born.

Oh, brilliant!

There's a sort of a cheer, although Bernie Mulligan is still upset he hasn't been asked to give some of his body fluid. We all repack our bags and stow stuff back in our lockers.

And on the top of mine there's still this pink envelope.

"Ye can open it now if ye want. No one will see. There's plenty goin' on."

She's right. No one gives a damn about Fiona Radcliffe any more. Except me. I smile – a really sick smile. Known as 'guilty as hell'. While Fiona watches me I open the envelope. But I've put my mind and my feelings into the freezer for a bit.

It's an invitation to a birthday treat. To go bowling with Fiona and her Mum on Saturday, then tea at Dizzy's Diner afterwards.

I can't say anything. There are no words in my head any more. Ask me my name and I'm going to struggle.

And there's worse to come. Tucked in the card is a slip of paper.

"Tha's what I didn't want found ..." she says. She laughs, a lovely little low laugh down in her throat. "Tha's dynamite!"

My fingers are jangling like a skeleton's as I open the note.

Dear Chrissy, (it says)

I hope you can come out with me on my birthday. You've been great to me and I like you a lot. The others have been crap but you've been kind. They hate me and I get the feeling you feel the opposite. You played me that love song. You don't treat me like you're going to catch something off me. Am I right? In case I am, let me tell you what I like about you. Really going out on a limb, I am!

Oh, dear God, the note goes on over the page. Almost with my eyes shut I have to read it. What she's written should make me hit the ceiling with joy. But as I read it, every word is like a whip lash across my back.

1. You've got kind eyes, Chrissy.

2. I like the way your hair's layered.

3. I listen for the little grunts in your throat when you're stuck over something.

4. And did you know, when you're thinking, your mouth pouts up a bit like you're going to kiss someone ...?

Now I do shut my eyes. What a total schmuk I've been. What a steaming heap of dung. What a traitor! Going to Henshaw and ratting on this girl because she put a secret love letter in my locker!

Please come! Kisses.

Fiona   XXXXX

I can't look up, I scrunch the note back into the card. I cram the card back into the envelope. I stuff the envelope into my pocket. Then there's no more delaying I can do.

So, "Ta," I say and start sorting my things. Busy, busy, busy. And 'ta' is a triumph to get out, I can tell you.

I never want to say anything to anyone ever again.

Chapter 7
The Thief of Love

Somehow I get through the afternoon without coming too close to Fiona. We have Games, which means the boys aren't with the girls, anyway.

I play the worst game of seven-a-side in my life. I can't midfield scheme my way through an open gate. I take ages getting changed and at the end of the day I scoot out of school and head off home like the dogs of hell are snapping at my backside.

I've never had a girl say things like that to me. I've never felt about anyone the way I feel about Fiona Radcliffe.

I started off thinking of her as a girl instead of as a person. Now she's a person miles high above being a girl. Except, her being a girl's no drawback. No, sir. But I know her as her. I like Fiona Radcliffe.

I love her.

And suddenly, she's walking next to me. She's seen me and run to catch me up.

"Chrissy! Chrissy Foreman!" She's with me, next to me on the pavement. "All right, Chrissy? Did I embarrass you? M'note? Is tha' why ...?"

I shake my head and walk on. I don't know what to say to her. And just at that moment Henshaw comes past us on his bike. He's left early to sort out his credit cards, no doubt.

And as he cycles past, he sees me and he sees Fiona with me. And he gives me such a look. There's a three movement symphony in that look. How can I be walking home with the girl I betrayed to him at breaktime? What sort of a creep am I?

He cycles on and Fiona stops. She's laid herself on the line in that note and I've still said nothing.

Suddenly she looks proud and defiant again, like she did on the day she first walked in. When everyone was against her. When I first fell head-over-heels. I stop, too.

"Well?" she asks.

I look her in the eye. It's the least I can do. But I know I don't deserve to lick her shoes. She's a million times too nice for a grasser like me.

"Ta for the invite," I say. "But I'm busy Saturday."

And I run off home to get to my room
and cry my eyes out.

Barrington Stoke would like to thank all its readers for commenting on the manuscript before publication and in particular:

Michael Carruthers
Craig Davidson
Jonathan Fern
Sam Gaskill
Philippa Georghiou
Carol Grainger
Hannah Williams

Become a Consultant!

Would you like to give us feedback on our titles before they are published? Contact us at the address or website below – we'd love to hear from you!

Barrington Stoke, 10 Belford Terrace, Edinburgh EH4 3DQ
Tel: 0131 315 4933 Fax: 0131 315 4934
E-mail: barringtonstoke@cs.com
Website: www.barringtonstoke.co.uk

More Titles

To Be A Millionaire
by Yvonne Coppard

The news that a famous film director is in town sets Jack's mind racing. At last, he thinks, he's finally got his break! All he has to do is to be in the right place at the right time. This time it's up to him.

The Shadow on The Stairs
by Ann Halam

People say Joe's new house is haunted. Every night, he looks for the shadow on the attic stairs. Sometimes he thinks he can see it, sometimes he knows he can't. He tells himself that he isn't scared and wishes he could get the idea that it is evil out of his mind ...

Runaway Teacher
by Pete Johnson

Scott thinks teachers are boring. Then a new teacher arrives - a teacher with very different ideas about lessons, rules and school. But when too many rules are broken, Scott learns just how complicated friendship and loyalty can be.

Falling Awake
by Viv French

Danny is cool. The younger kids think they're cool too, but they are just kiddie babes to Danny. He can make easy money out of them. He isn't going to say no to easy money, is he? Not until the day he wakes up on the pavement. Out of it. Trapped. This time Danny's gone too far.

Alien Deeps
by Douglas Hill

When Tal plunges through the protecting field on the edge of the Clear Zone, he knows that he is leaving the only safe place on the planet. Beyond it lies the unknown, a world outside human control. But is the unknown the greatest danger in the alien deeps?